P9-DEW-287

THIS CANDLEWICK BOOK BELONGS TO:

First paperback edition 2003

The Library of Congress has cataloged the hardcover edition as follows:
Masurel, Claire.
Two homes / Claire Masurel ; illustrated by Kady MacDonald Denton. —1st ed.
p. cm.
Summary: A young boy named Alex enjoys the homes of both of his parents who live apart but love Alex very much.
ISBN 0-7636-0511-5 (hardcover)
[1. Divorce—Fiction. 2. Parent and child—Fiction. 3. Dwellings—Fiction.]
I. Denton, Kady MacDonald, ill. II. Title.
PZ7.M4239584 Tw 2001
[E]—dc21 00-041398
ISBN 0-7636-1984-1 (paperback)

6 8 10 9 7

Printed in China

This book was typeset in Godlike.
The illustrations were done in ink, watercolor, and gouache.

Candlewick Press
2067 Massachusetts Avenue
Cambridge, Massachusetts 02140

visit us at www.candlewick.com

Two Homes

Claire Masurel illustrated by Kady MacDonald Denton

CANDLEWICK PRESS
CAMBRIDGE, MASSACHUSETTS

Here I am! I am Alex.

This is Daddy.

And this is Mommy.

Daddy lives here.
Sometimes I'm with Daddy.

Mommy lives there.
Sometimes I'm with Mommy.

So . . . I have *two homes!*

I have *two* front doors.

My coat goes here.

My coat goes there.

I have *two* rooms.

My room at Daddy's.

My room at Mommy's.

I have *two* favorite chairs.

A rocking chair at Daddy's.

A soft chair at Mommy's.

I have lots of friends.

Friends come and play at Daddy's.

Friends come and play at Mommy's.

I have *two* kitchens.

Daddy and I cook here.

Mommy and I cook there.

I have *two* bathrooms.

I have a toothbrush at Daddy's.

I have a toothbrush at Mommy's.

And I have *two* telephone numbers.

Mommy calls me at Daddy's house.

Daddy calls me at Mommy's house.

I love Daddy.

And I love Mommy.
No matter where I am.

We love you, Alex.

We love you wherever we are.

And we love you wherever YOU *are.*